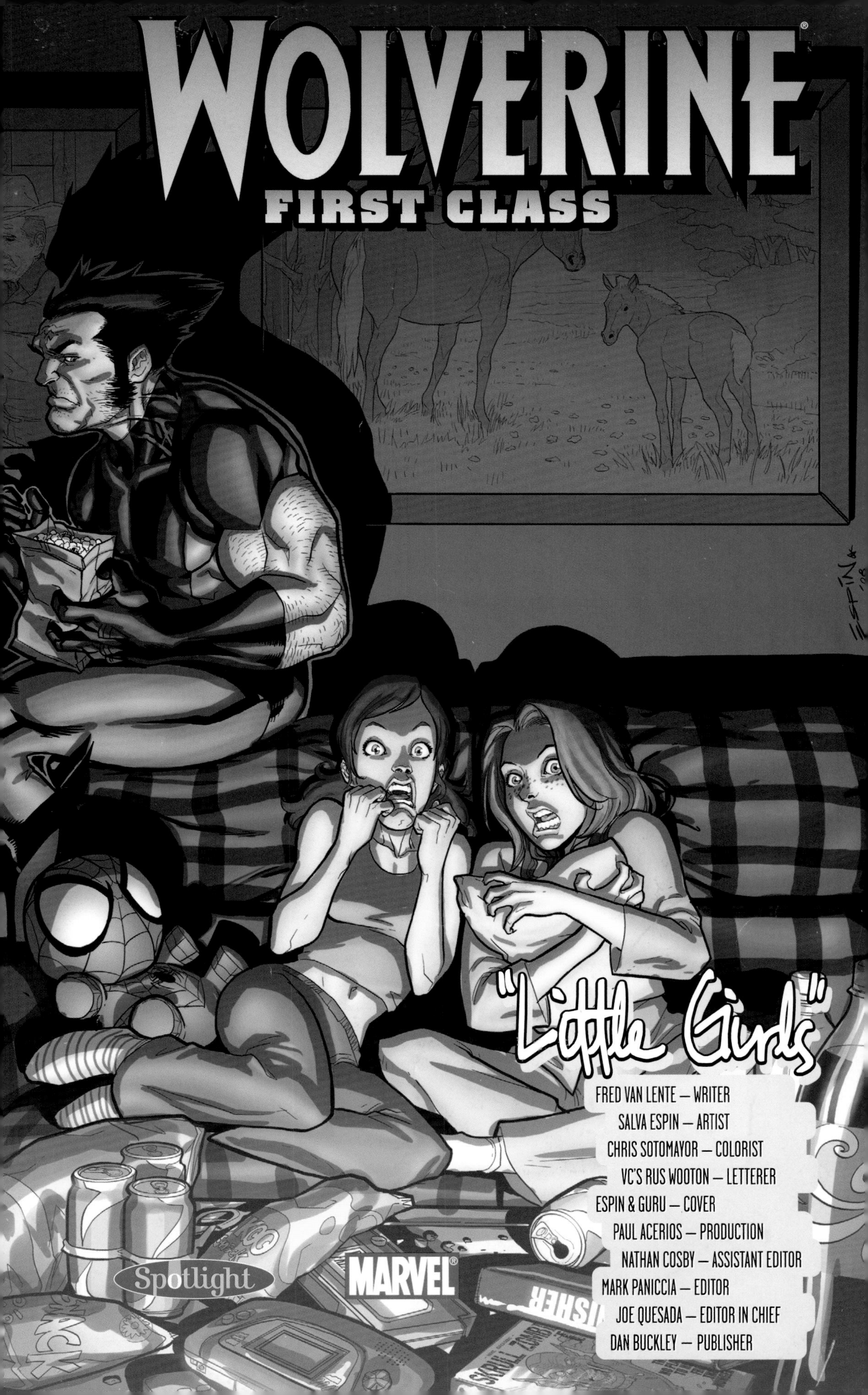
WOLVERINE®
FIRST CLASS
"Little Girls"
FRED VAN LENTE – WRITER
SALVA ESPIN – ARTIST
CHRIS SOTOMAYOR – COLORIST
VC'S RUS WOOTON – LETTERER
ESPIN & GURU – COVER
PAUL ACERIOS – PRODUCTION
NATHAN COSBY – ASSISTANT EDITOR
MARK PANICCIA – EDITOR
JOE QUESADA – EDITOR IN CHIEF
DAN BUCKLEY – PUBLISHER
Spotlight
MARVEL®

VISIT US AT
www.abdopublishing.com

Reinforced library bound edition published in 2010 by Spotlight, a division of the ABDO Group, 8000 West 78th Street, Edina, Minnesota 55439. Spotlight produces high-quality reinforced library bound editions for schools and libraries. Published by agreement with Marvel Characters, Inc.

Library of Congress Cataloging-in-Publication Data

Van Lente, Fred.
  Little girls / Fred Van Lente, writer ; Salva Espin, artist ; Chris Sotomayor, colorist ; Rus Wooton, letterer. -- Reinforced library bound ed.
     p. cm.
  "Marvel."
  ISBN 978-1-59961-673-5
 1. Graphic novels. 2. Graphic novels. [1. Graphic novels. 2. Superheroes--Fiction.] I. Espin, Salva, ill. II. Sotomayor, Chris. III. Wooton, Rus. IV. Title.
  PZ7.7.V26Li 2009
  741.5'973--dc22
                                      2009010138

All Spotlight books have reinforced library bindings and
are manufactured in the United States of America.

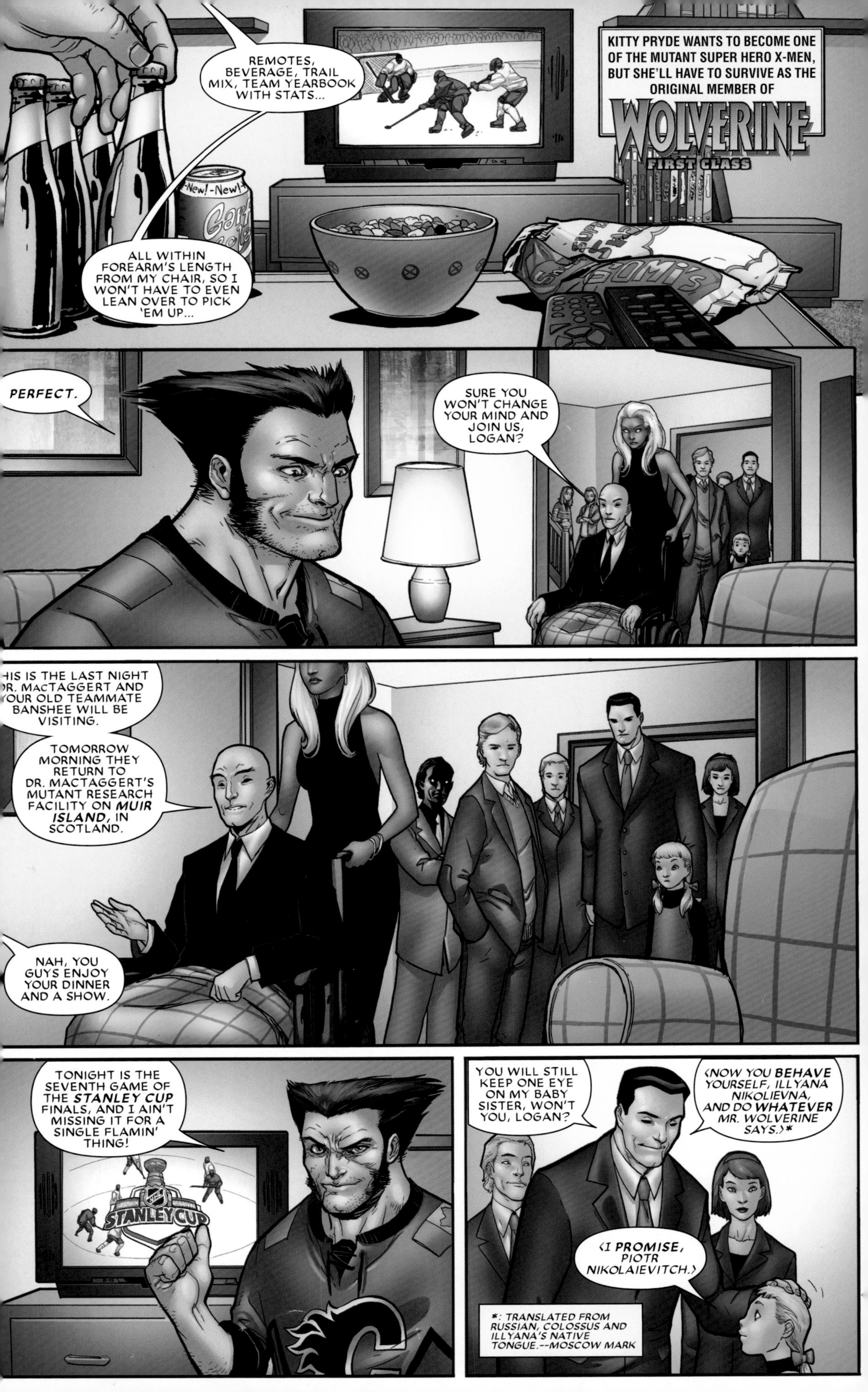

KITTY PRYDE WANTS TO BECOME ONE OF THE MUTANT SUPER HERO X-MEN, BUT SHE'LL HAVE TO SURVIVE AS THE ORIGINAL MEMBER OF
WOLVERINE FIRST CLASS
REMOTES, BEVERAGE, TRAIL MIX, TEAM YEARBOOK WITH STATS...
ALL WITHIN FOREARM'S LENGTH FROM MY CHAIR, SO I WON'T HAVE TO EVEN LEAN OVER TO PICK 'EM UP...
PERFECT.
SURE YOU WON'T CHANGE YOUR MIND AND JOIN US, LOGAN?
HIS IS THE LAST NIGHT R. MacTAGGERT AND OUR OLD TEAMMATE BANSHEE WILL BE VISITING.
TOMORROW MORNING THEY RETURN TO DR. MACTAGGERT'S MUTANT RESEARCH FACILITY ON MUIR ISLAND, IN SCOTLAND.
NAH, YOU GUYS ENJOY YOUR DINNER AND A SHOW.
TONIGHT IS THE SEVENTH GAME OF THE STANLEY CUP FINALS, AND I AIN'T MISSING IT FOR A SINGLE FLAMIN' THING!
STANLEY CUP
YOU WILL STILL KEEP ONE EYE ON MY BABY SISTER, WON'T YOU, LOGAN?
‹NOW YOU BEHAVE YOURSELF, ILLYANA NIKOLIEVNA, AND DO WHATEVER MR. WOLVERINE SAYS.›*
‹I PROMISE, PIOTR NIKOLAIEVITCH.›
*: TRANSLATED FROM RUSSIAN, COLOSSUS AND ILLYANA'S NATIVE TONGUE.--MOSCOW MARK

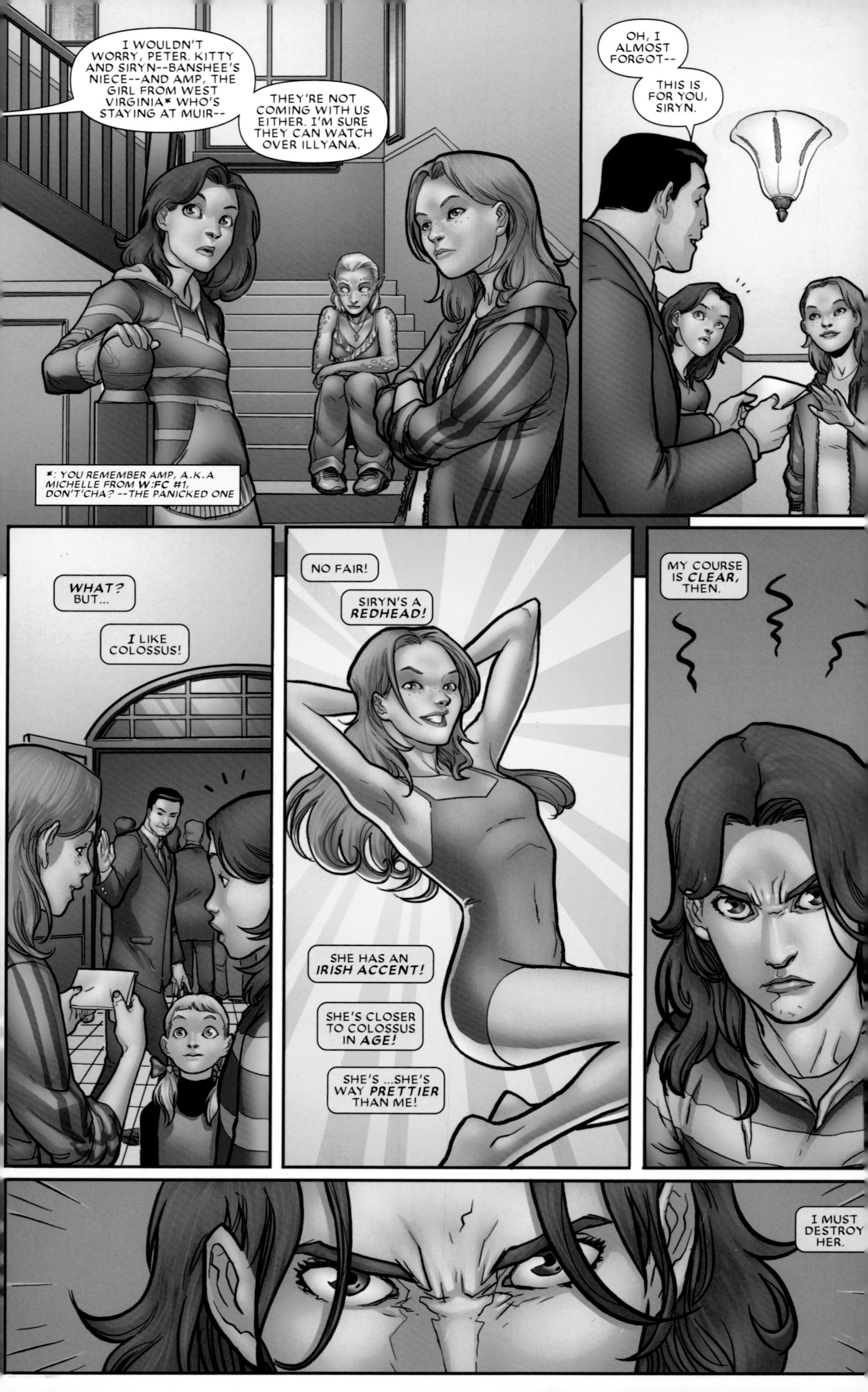

I WOULDN'T WORRY, PETER. KITTY AND SIRYN--BANSHEE'S NIECE--AND AMP, THE GIRL FROM WEST VIRGINIA* WHO'S STAYING AT MUIR--
THEY'RE NOT COMING WITH US EITHER. I'M SURE THEY CAN WATCH OVER ILLYANA.
*: YOU REMEMBER AMP, A.K.A MICHELLE FROM W:FC #1, DON'T'CHA? --THE PANICKED ONE
OH, I ALMOST FORGOT--
THIS IS FOR YOU, SIRYN.
WHAT? BUT...
I LIKE COLOSSUS!
NO FAIR!
SIRYN'S A REDHEAD!
SHE HAS AN IRISH ACCENT!
SHE'S CLOSER TO COLOSSUS IN AGE!
SHE'S ...SHE'S WAY PRETTIER THAN ME!
MY COURSE IS CLEAR, THEN.
I MUST DESTROY HER.

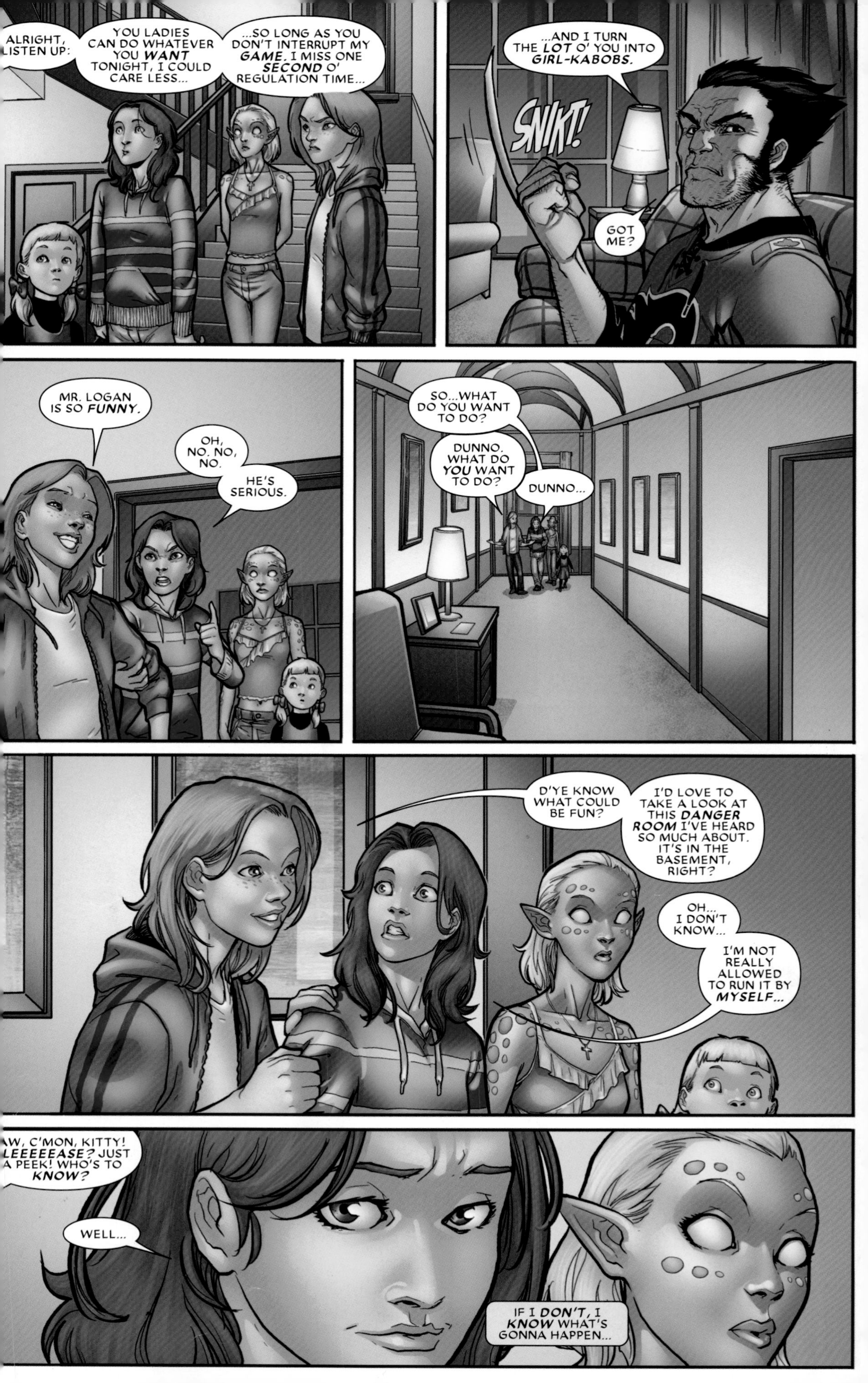
ALRIGHT, LISTEN UP:
YOU LADIES CAN DO WHATEVER YOU WANT TONIGHT, I COULD CARE LESS...
...SO LONG AS YOU DON'T INTERRUPT MY GAME. I MISS ONE SECOND O' REGULATION TIME...
...AND I TURN THE LOT O' YOU INTO GIRL-KABOBS.
SNIKT!
GOT ME?
MR. LOGAN IS SO FUNNY.
OH, NO. NO, NO.
HE'S SERIOUS.
SO...WHAT DO YOU WANT TO DO?
DUNNO. WHAT DO YOU WANT TO DO?
DUNNO...
D'YE KNOW WHAT COULD BE FUN?
I'D LOVE TO TAKE A LOOK AT THIS DANGER ROOM I'VE HEARD SO MUCH ABOUT. IT'S IN THE BASEMENT, RIGHT?
OH... I DON'T KNOW...
I'M NOT REALLY ALLOWED TO RUN IT BY MYSELF...
W, C'MON, KITTY! LEEEEEASE? JUST A PEEK! WHO'S TO KNOW?
WELL...
IF I DON'T, I KNOW WHAT'S GONNA HAPPEN...

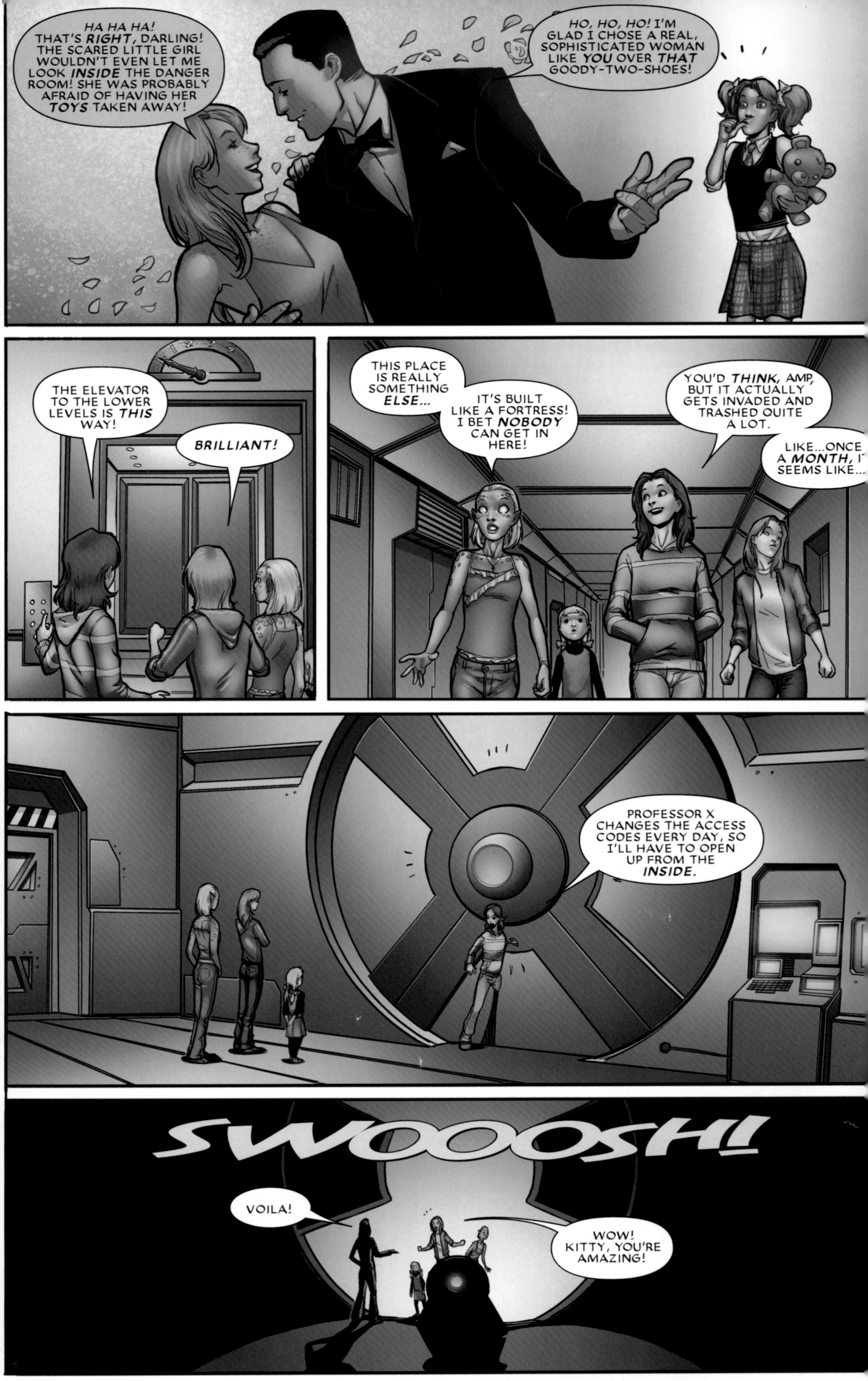

HA HA HA! THAT'S RIGHT, DARLING! THE SCARED LITTLE GIRL WOULDN'T EVEN LET ME LOOK INSIDE THE DANGER ROOM! SHE WAS PROBABLY AFRAID OF HAVING HER TOYS TAKEN AWAY!
HO, HO, HO! I'M GLAD I CHOSE A REAL, SOPHISTICATED WOMAN LIKE YOU OVER THAT GOODY-TWO-SHOES!
THE ELEVATOR TO THE LOWER LEVELS IS THIS WAY!
BRILLIANT!
THIS PLACE IS REALLY SOMETHING ELSE...
IT'S BUILT LIKE A FORTRESS! I BET NOBODY CAN GET IN HERE!
YOU'D THINK, AMP, BUT IT ACTUALLY GETS INVADED AND TRASHED QUITE A LOT.
LIKE...ONCE A MONTH, I SEEMS LIKE...
PROFESSOR X CHANGES THE ACCESS CODES EVERY DAY, SO I'LL HAVE TO OPEN UP FROM THE INSIDE.
SWOOOSH!
VOILA!
WOW! KITTY, YOU'RE AMAZING!

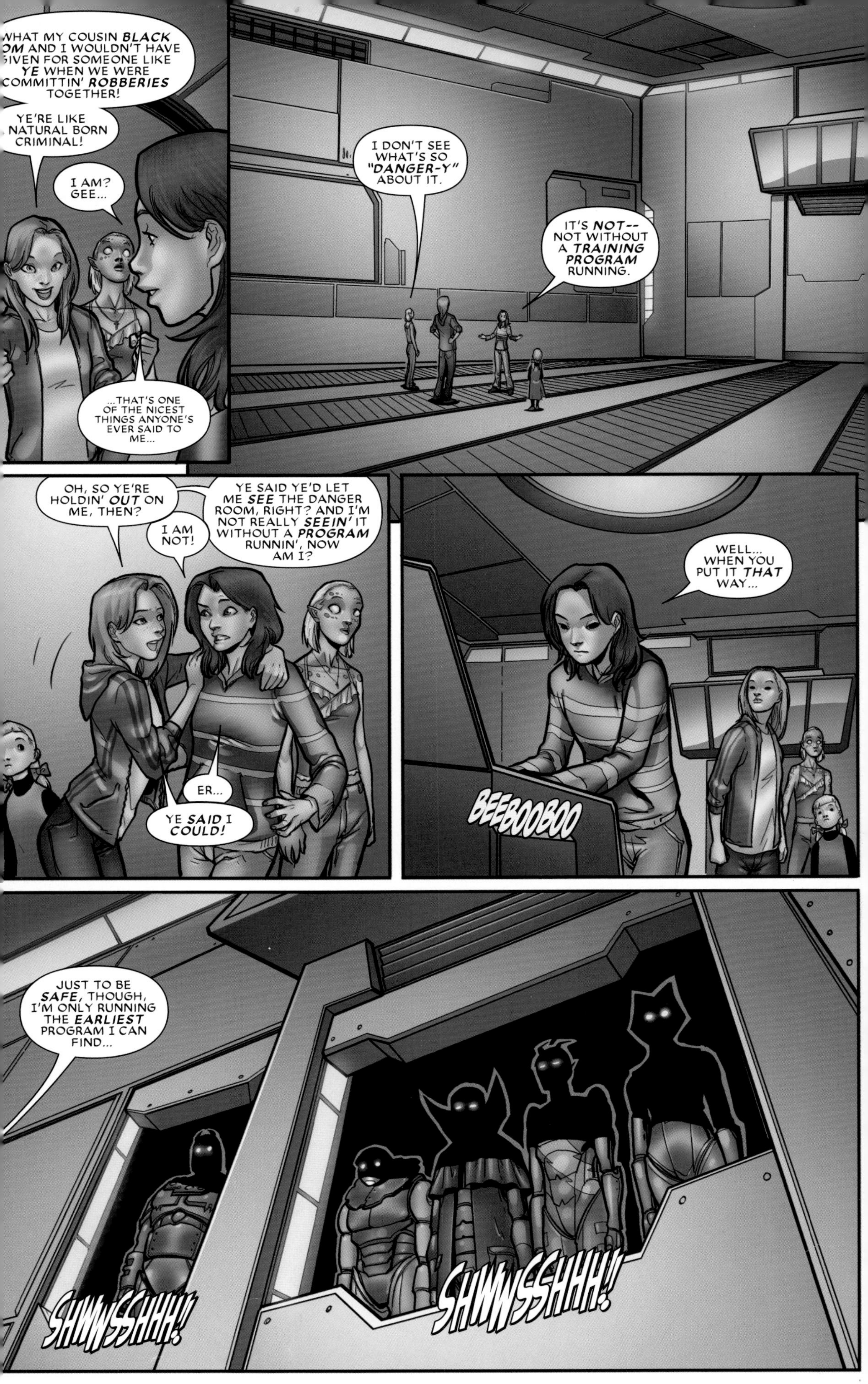
WHAT MY COUSIN BLACK TOM AND I WOULDN'T HAVE GIVEN FOR SOMEONE LIKE YE WHEN WE WERE COMMITTIN' ROBBERIES TOGETHER!
YE'RE LIKE NATURAL BORN CRIMINAL!
I AM? GEE...
...THAT'S ONE OF THE NICEST THINGS ANYONE'S EVER SAID TO ME...
I DON'T SEE WHAT'S SO "DANGER-Y" ABOUT IT.
IT'S NOT-- NOT WITHOUT A TRAINING PROGRAM RUNNING.
OH, SO YE'RE HOLDIN' OUT ON ME, THEN?
I AM NOT!
YE SAID YE'D LET ME SEE THE DANGER ROOM, RIGHT? AND I'M NOT REALLY SEEIN' IT WITHOUT A PROGRAM RUNNIN', NOW AM I?
ER...
YE SAID I COULD!
WELL... WHEN YOU PUT IT THAT WAY...
BEEBOOBOO
JUST TO BE SAFE, THOUGH, I'M ONLY RUNNING THE EARLIEST PROGRAM I CAN FIND...
SHWWSSHHH!!
SHWWSSHHH!!

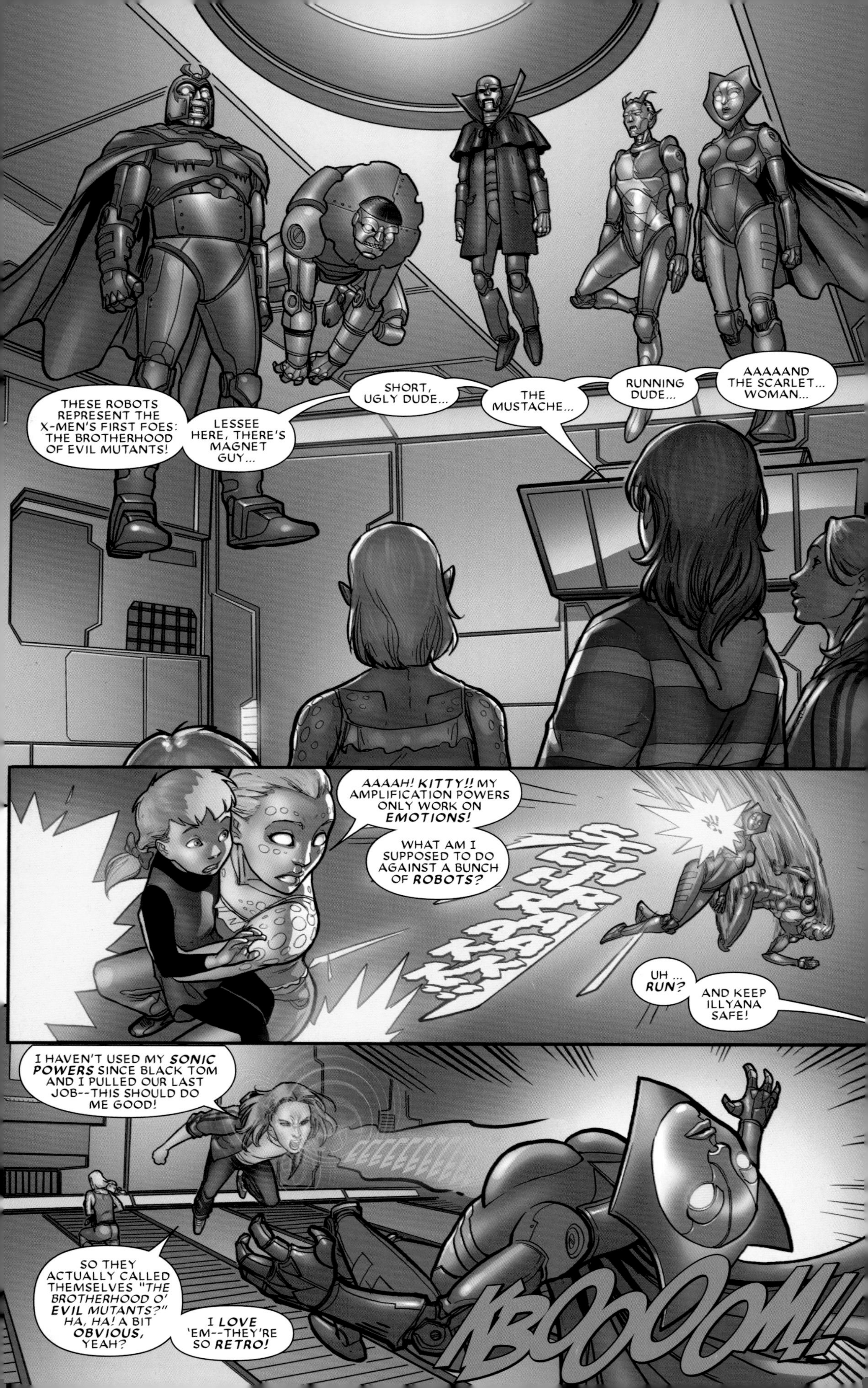
THESE ROBOTS REPRESENT THE X-MEN'S FIRST FOES: THE BROTHERHOOD OF EVIL MUTANTS!
LESSEE HERE, THERE'S MAGNET GUY...
SHORT, UGLY DUDE...
THE MUSTACHE...
RUNNING DUDE...
AAAAAND THE SCARLET... WOMAN...
AAAAH! KITTY!! MY AMPLIFICATION POWERS ONLY WORK ON EMOTIONS!
WHAT AM I SUPPOSED TO DO AGAINST A BUNCH OF ROBOTS?
UH ... RUN?
AND KEEP ILLYANA SAFE!
I HAVEN'T USED MY SONIC POWERS SINCE BLACK TOM AND I PULLED OUR LAST JOB--THIS SHOULD DO ME GOOD!
EEEEEEEEEE
SO THEY ACTUALLY CALLED THEMSELVES "THE BROTHERHOOD O' EVIL MUTANTS?" HA, HA! A BIT OBVIOUS, YEAH?
I LOVE 'EM--THEY'RE SO RETRO!
KBOOOOM!!

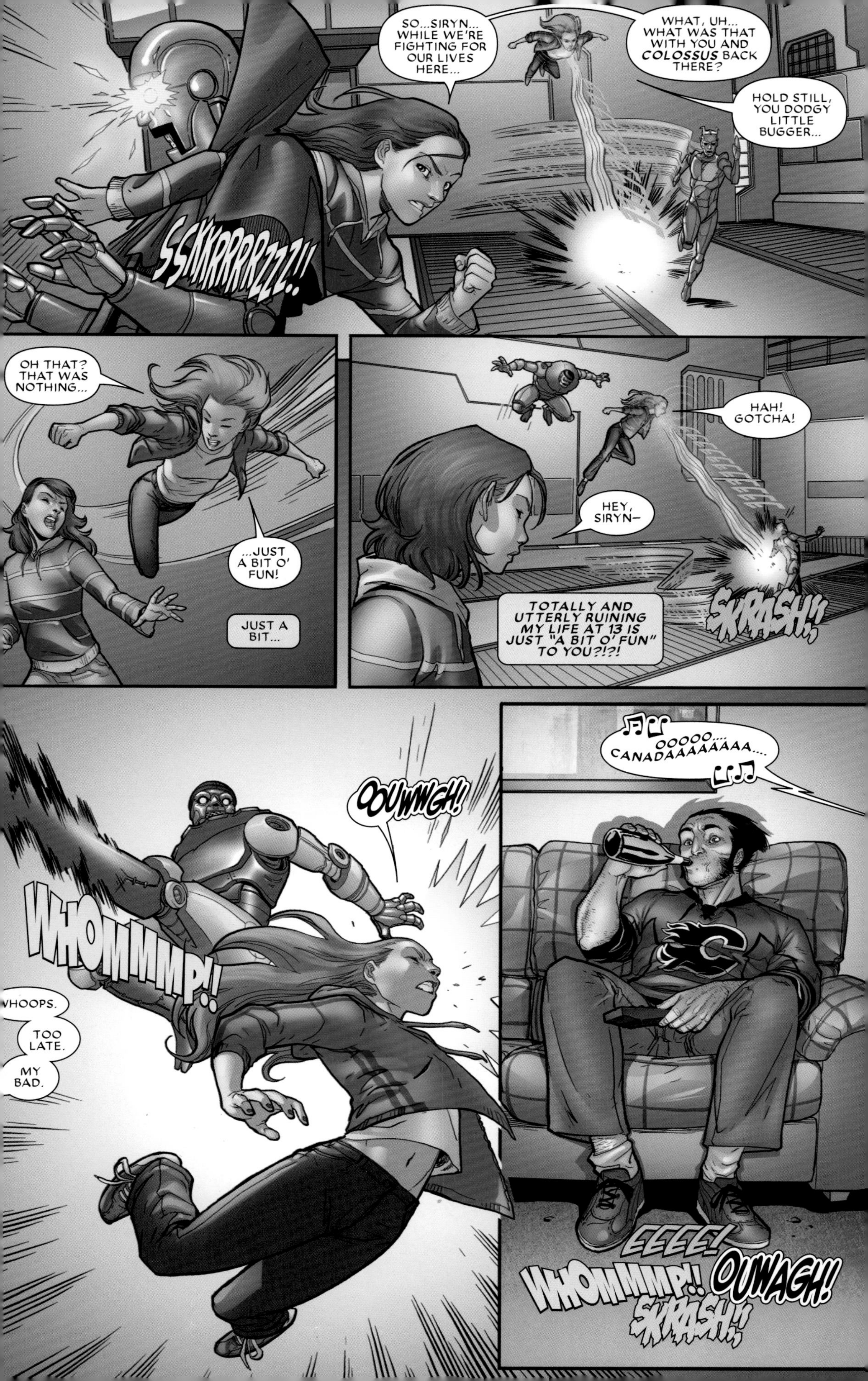
SO...SIRYN... WHILE WE'RE FIGHTING FOR OUR LIVES HERE...
WHAT, UH... WHAT WAS THAT WITH YOU AND COLOSSUS BACK THERE?
HOLD STILL, YOU DODGY LITTLE BUGGER...
SSKKRRRRZZZ!!
OH THAT? THAT WAS NOTHING...
...JUST A BIT O' FUN!
JUST A BIT...
HAH! GOTCHA!
HEY, SIRYN–
TOTALLY AND UTTERLY RUINING MY LIFE AT 13 IS JUST "A BIT O' FUN" TO YOU?!?!
SKRASH!!
OOUWWGH!
WHOMMMMP!!
WHOOPS.
TOO LATE.
MY BAD.
OOOOO.... CANADAAAAAAAA....
EEEE!
WHOMMMP!!
OUWAGH!
SKRASH!!

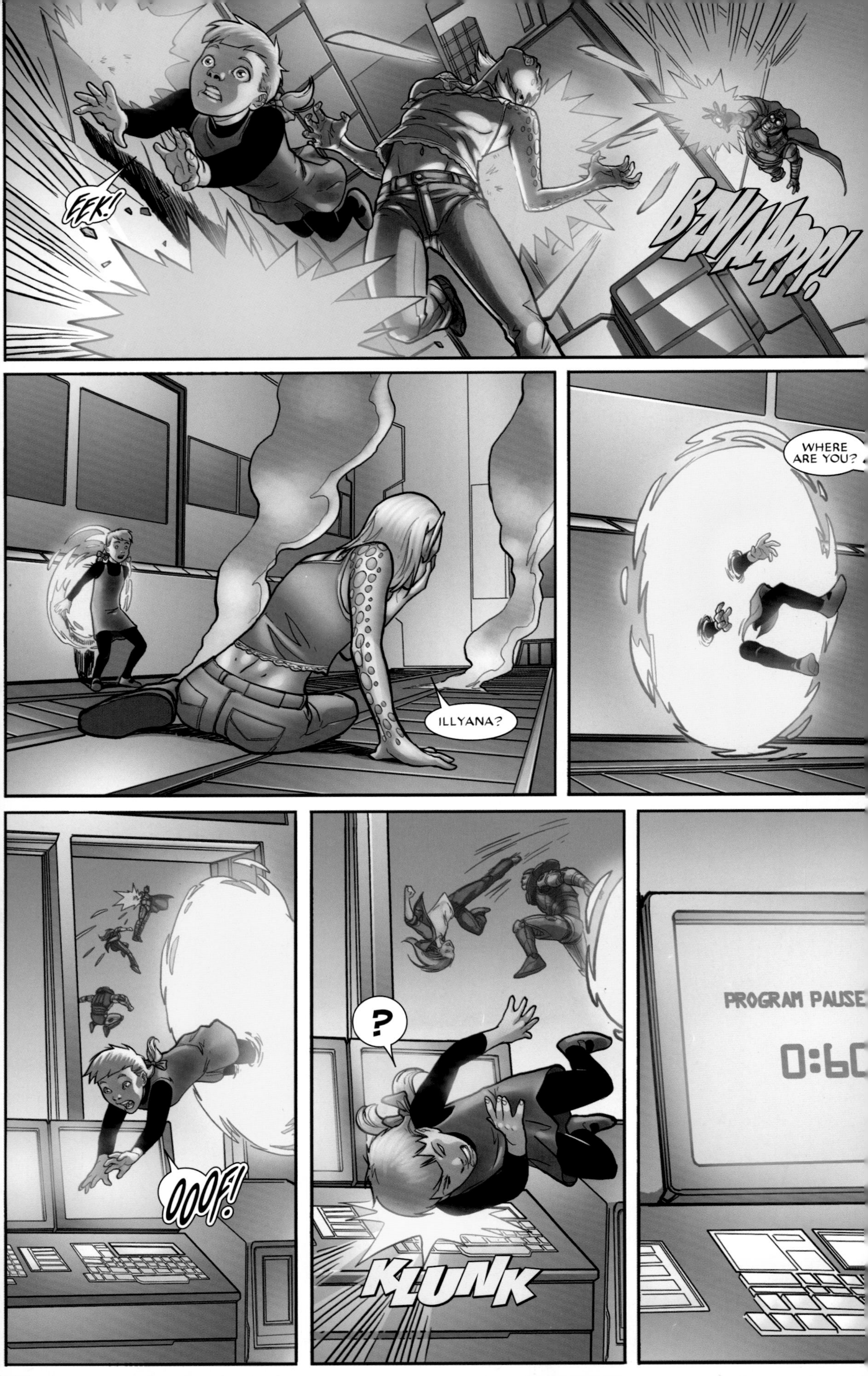
EEK!
BWAAPP!
ILLYANA?
WHERE ARE YOU?
OOOF!
?
KLUNK
PROGRAM PAUSE
0:60

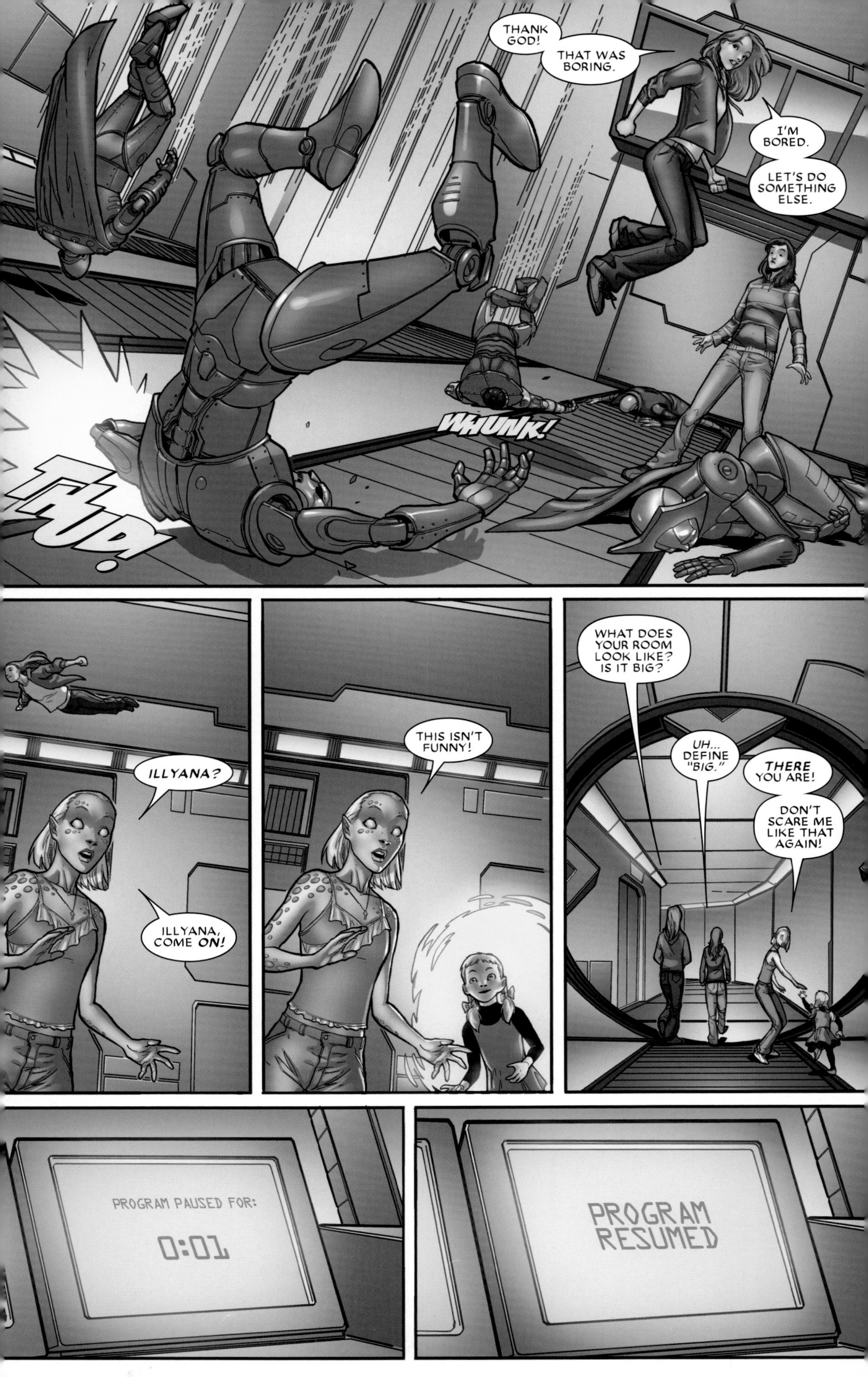
THANK GOD!
THAT WAS BORING.
I'M BORED.
LET'S DO SOMETHING ELSE.
THUD!
WHUNK!
ILLYANA?
ILLYANA, COME ON!
THIS ISN'T FUNNY!
WHAT DOES YOUR ROOM LOOK LIKE? IS IT BIG?
UH... DEFINE "BIG."
THERE YOU ARE!
DON'T SCARE ME LIKE THAT AGAIN!
PROGRAM PAUSED FOR:
0:01
PROGRAM RESUMED

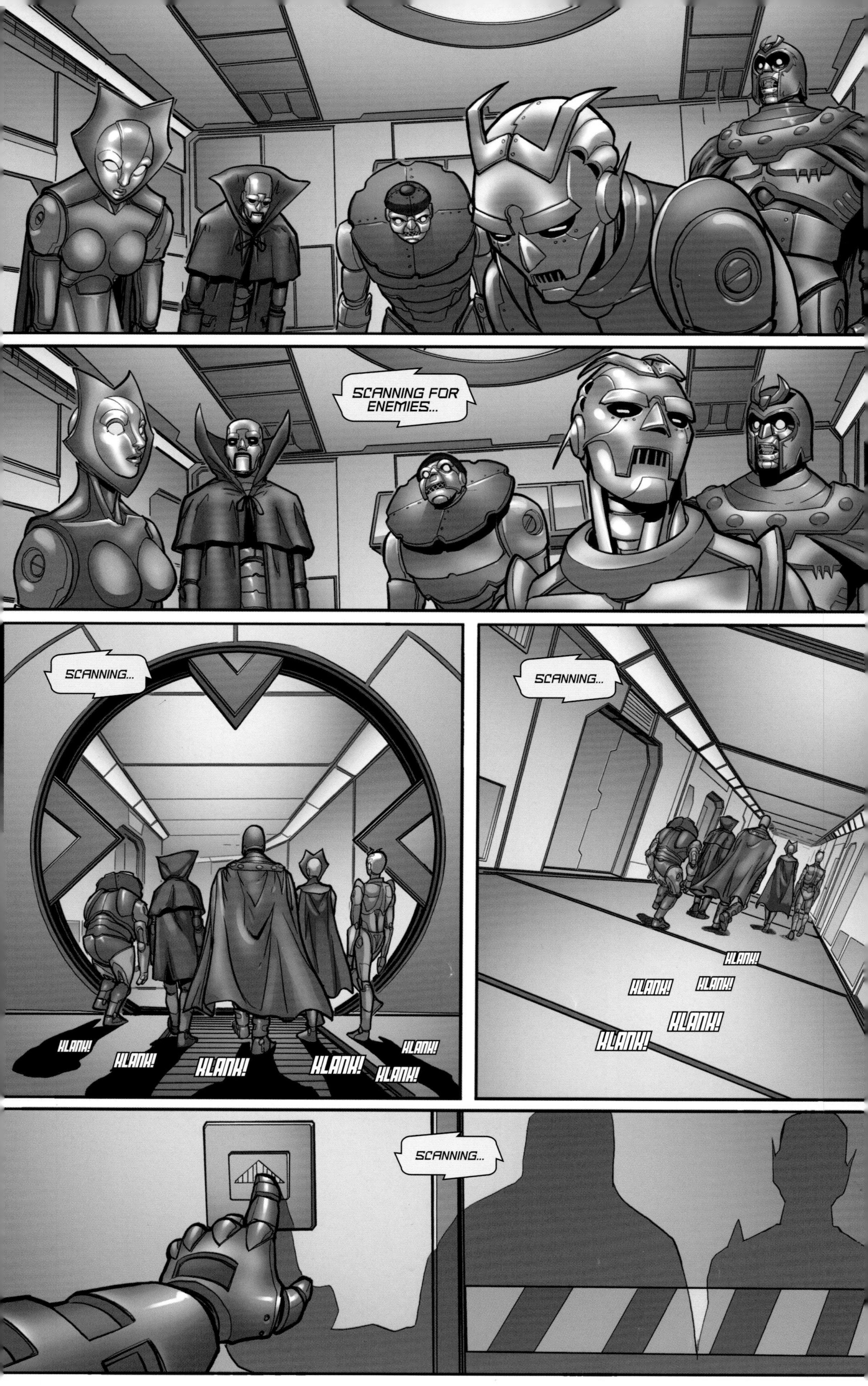
SCANNING FOR ENEMIES...
SCANNING...
KLANK!
KLANK!
KLANK!
KLANK!
KLANK!
KLANK!
SCANNING...
KLANK!
KLANK!
KLANK!
KLANK!
KLANK!
SCANNING...

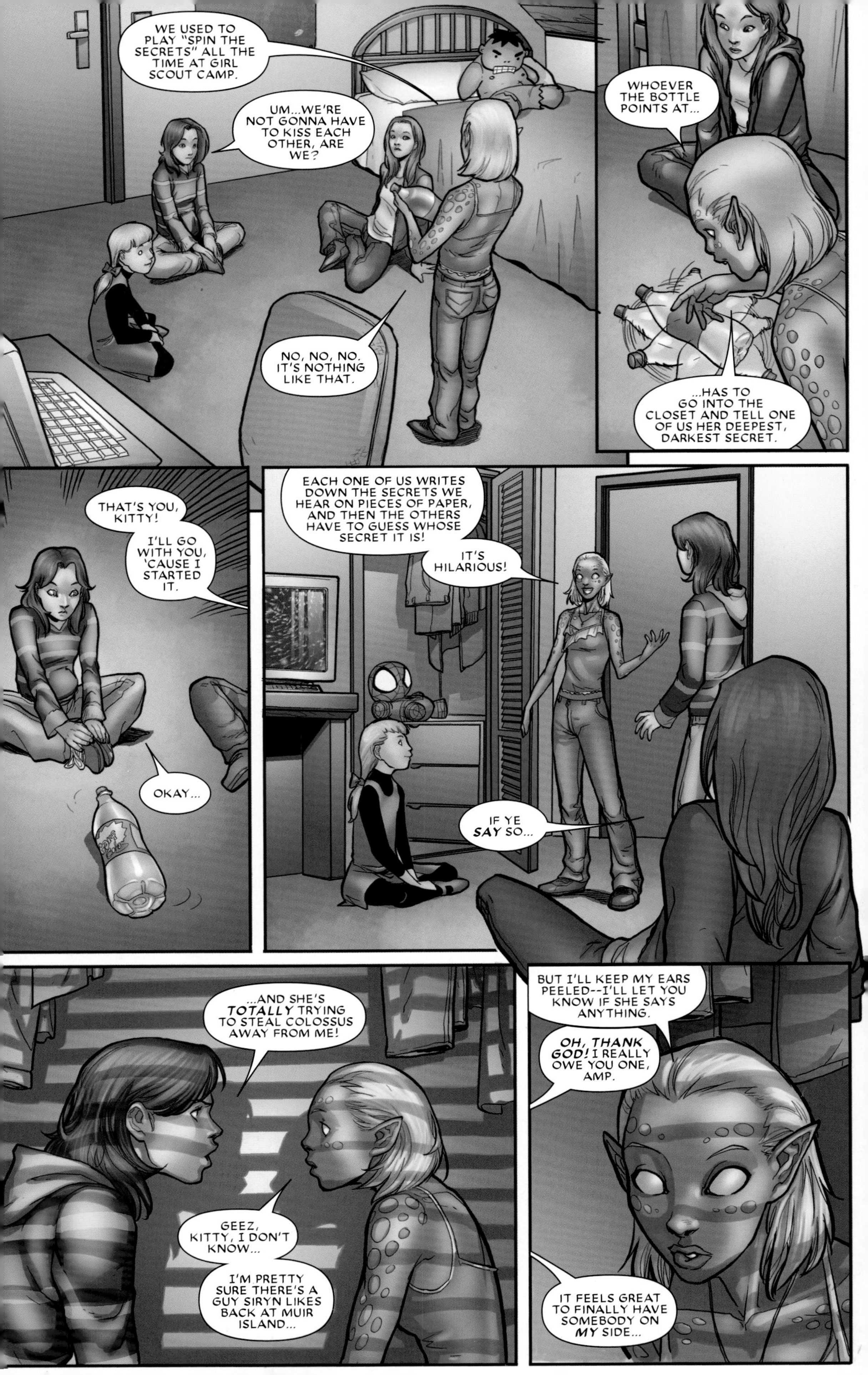
WE USED TO PLAY "SPIN THE SECRETS" ALL THE TIME AT GIRL SCOUT CAMP.
UM...WE'RE NOT GONNA HAVE TO KISS EACH OTHER, ARE WE?
NO, NO, NO. IT'S NOTHING LIKE THAT.
WHOEVER THE BOTTLE POINTS AT...
...HAS TO GO INTO THE CLOSET AND TELL ONE OF US HER DEEPEST, DARKEST SECRET.
THAT'S YOU, KITTY!
I'LL GO WITH YOU, 'CAUSE I STARTED IT.
OKAY...
EACH ONE OF US WRITES DOWN THE SECRETS WE HEAR ON PIECES OF PAPER, AND THEN THE OTHERS HAVE TO GUESS WHOSE SECRET IT IS!
IT'S HILARIOUS!
IF YE *SAY* SO...
...AND SHE'S *TOTALLY* TRYING TO STEAL COLOSSUS AWAY FROM ME!
GEEZ, KITTY, I DON'T KNOW...
I'M PRETTY SURE THERE'S A GUY SIRYN LIKES BACK AT MUIR ISLAND...
BUT I'LL KEEP MY EARS PEELED--I'LL LET YOU KNOW IF SHE SAYS ANYTHING.
OH, THANK GOD! I REALLY OWE YOU ONE, AMP.
IT FEELS GREAT TO FINALLY HAVE SOMEBODY ON *MY* SIDE...

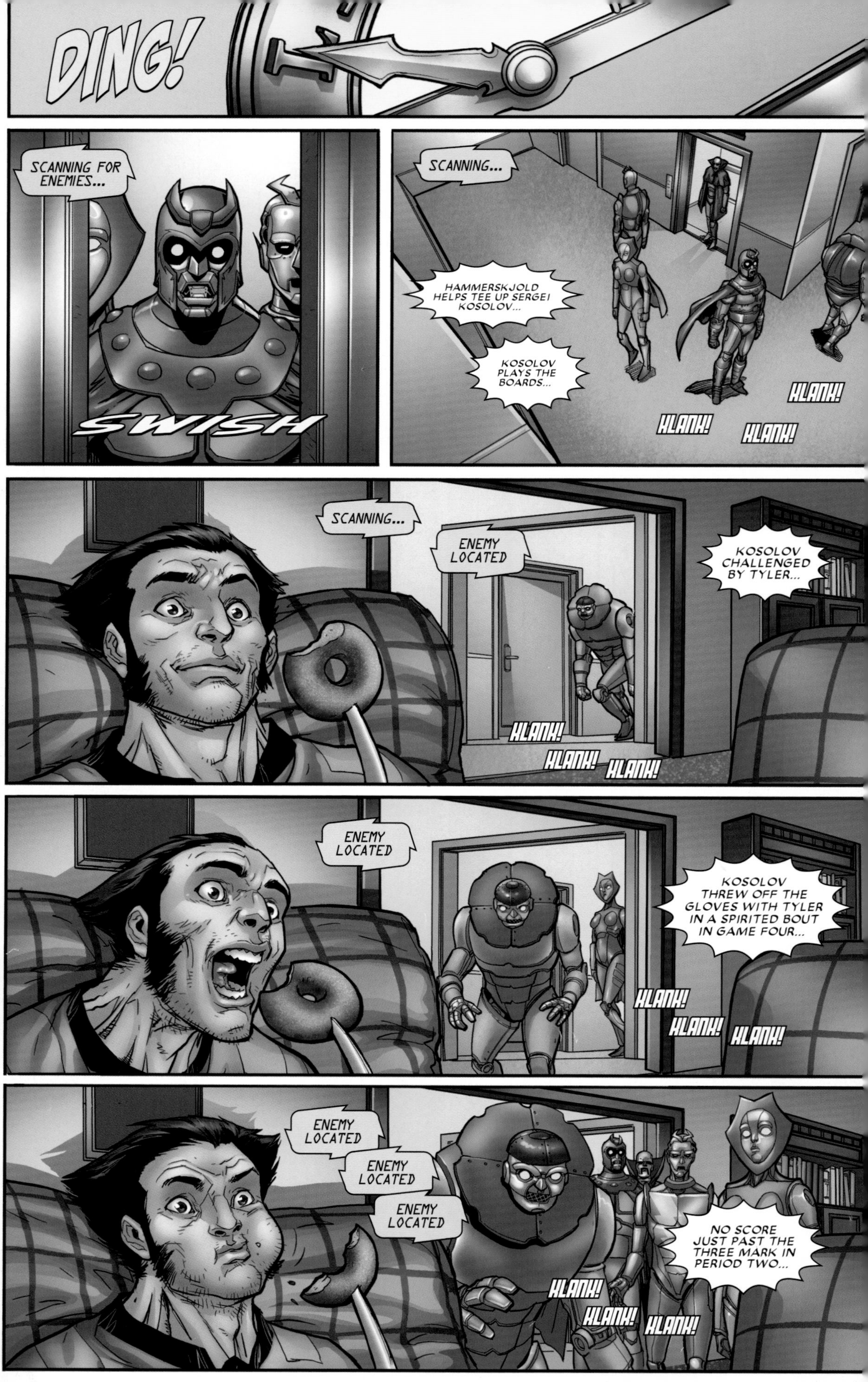
DING!
SCANNING FOR ENEMIES...
SWISH
SCANNING...
HAMMERSKJOLD HELPS TEE UP SERGEI KOSOLOV...
KOSOLOV PLAYS THE BOARDS...
KLANK!
KLANK!
KLANK!
SCANNING...
ENEMY LOCATED
KOSOLOV CHALLENGED BY TYLER...
KLANK!
KLANK!
KLANK!
ENEMY LOCATED
KOSOLOV THREW OFF THE GLOVES WITH TYLER IN A SPIRITED BOUT IN GAME FOUR...
KLANK!
KLANK!
KLANK!
ENEMY LOCATED
ENEMY LOCATED
ENEMY LOCATED
NO SCORE JUST PAST THE THREE MARK IN PERIOD TWO...
KLANK!
KLANK!
KLANK!

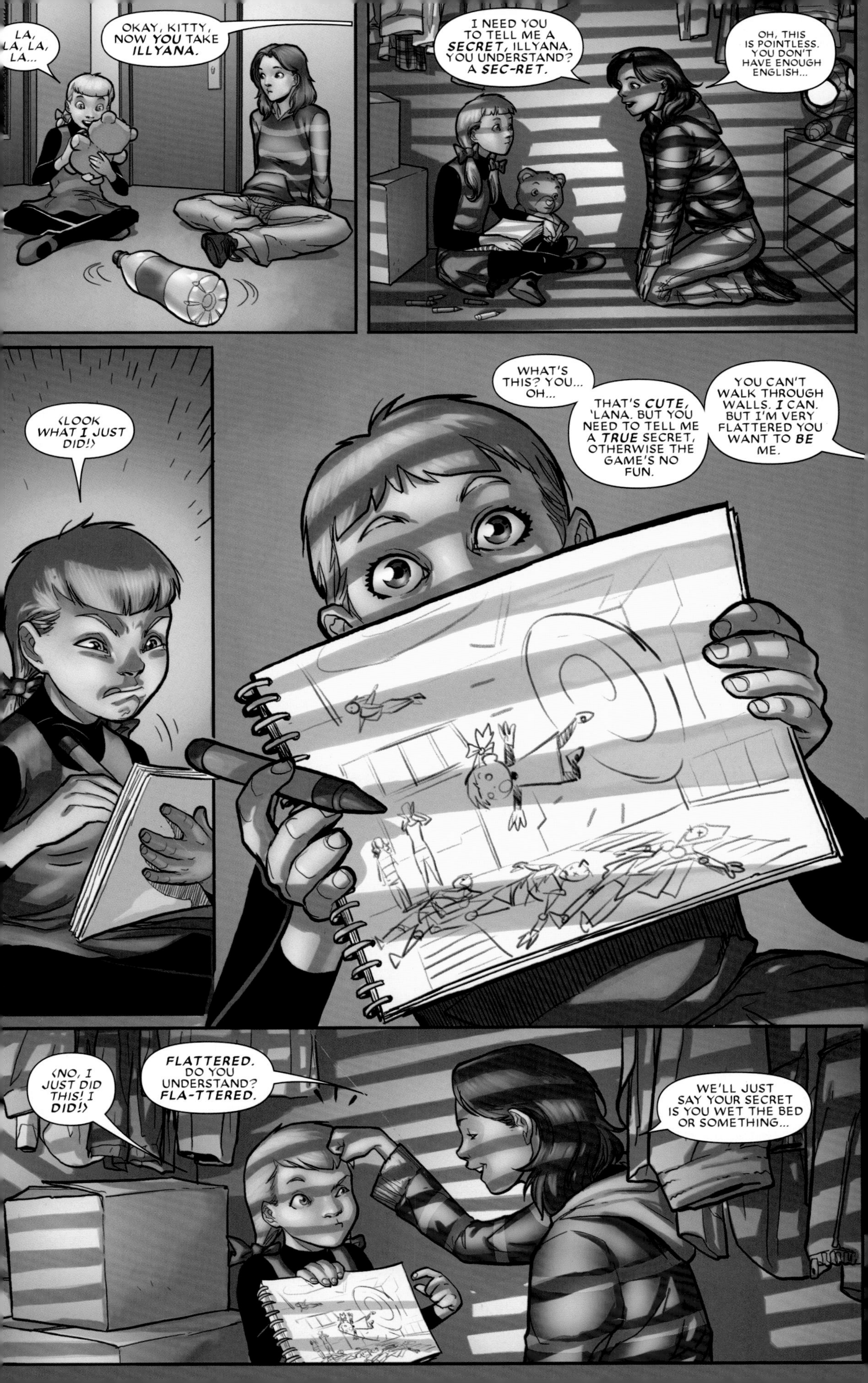
LA, LA, LA, LA...
OKAY, KITTY, NOW YOU TAKE ILLYANA.
I NEED YOU TO TELL ME A SECRET, ILLYANA. YOU UNDERSTAND? A SEC-RET.
OH, THIS IS POINTLESS. YOU DON'T HAVE ENOUGH ENGLISH...
<LOOK WHAT I JUST DID!>
WHAT'S THIS? YOU... OH...
THAT'S CUTE, 'LANA. BUT YOU NEED TO TELL ME A TRUE SECRET, OTHERWISE THE GAME'S NO FUN.
YOU CAN'T WALK THROUGH WALLS. I CAN. BUT I'M VERY FLATTERED YOU WANT TO BE ME.
<NO, I JUST DID THIS! I DID!>
FLATTERED. DO YOU UNDERSTAND? FLA-TTERED.
WE'LL JUST SAY YOUR SECRET IS YOU WET THE BED OR SOMETHING...

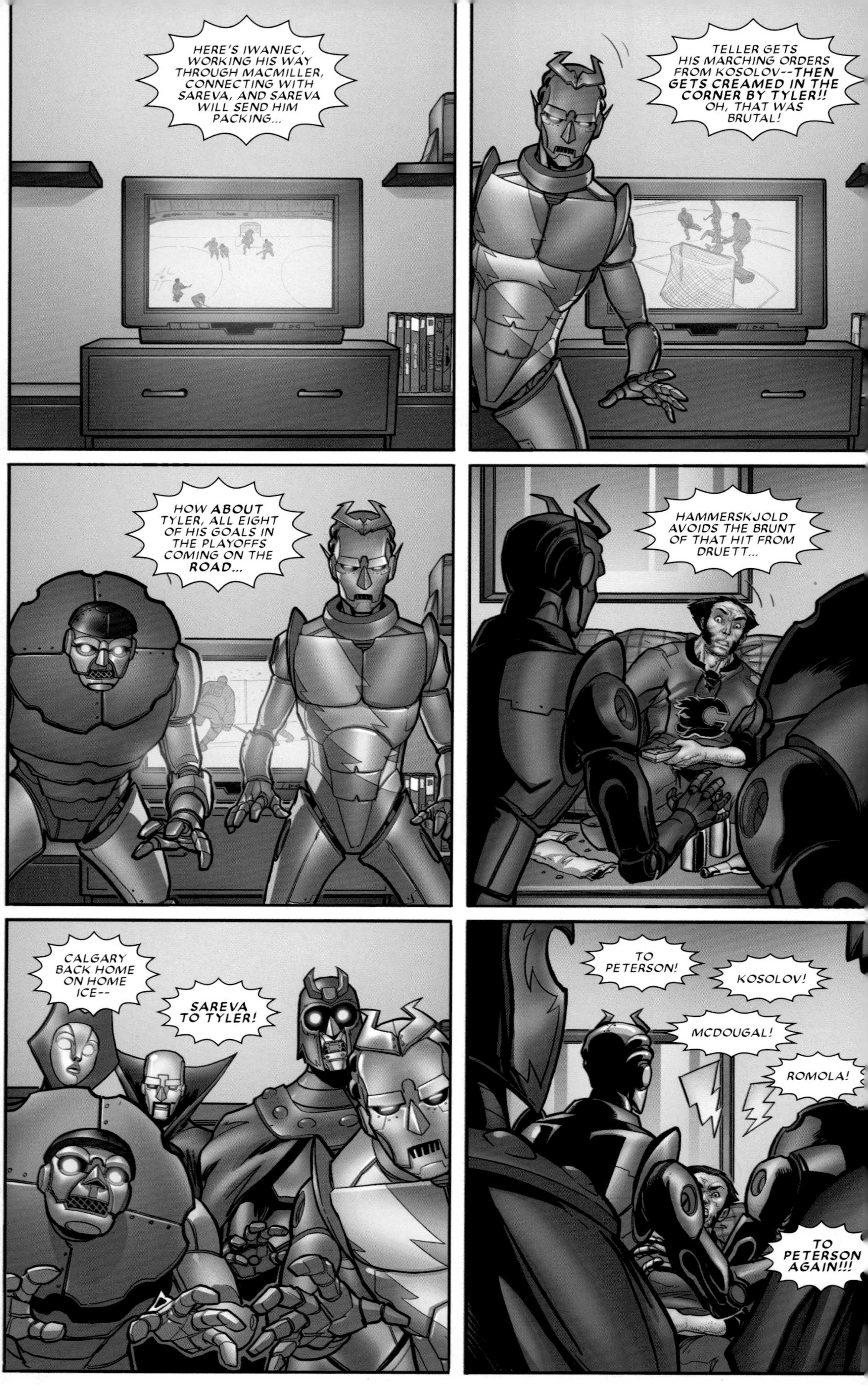
HERE'S IWANIEC, WORKING HIS WAY THROUGH MACMILLER, CONNECTING WITH SAREVA, AND SAREVA WILL SEND HIM PACKING...
TELLER GETS HIS MARCHING ORDERS FROM KOSOLOV--THEN GETS CREAMED IN THE CORNER BY TYLER!! OH, THAT WAS BRUTAL!
HOW ABOUT TYLER, ALL EIGHT OF HIS GOALS IN THE PLAYOFFS COMING ON THE ROAD...
HAMMERSKJOLD AVOIDS THE BRUNT OF THAT HIT FROM DRUETT...
CALGARY BACK HOME ON HOME ICE--
SAREVA TO TYLER!
TO PETERSON!
KOSOLOV!
MCDOUGAL!
ROMOLA!
TO PETERSON AGAIN!!!

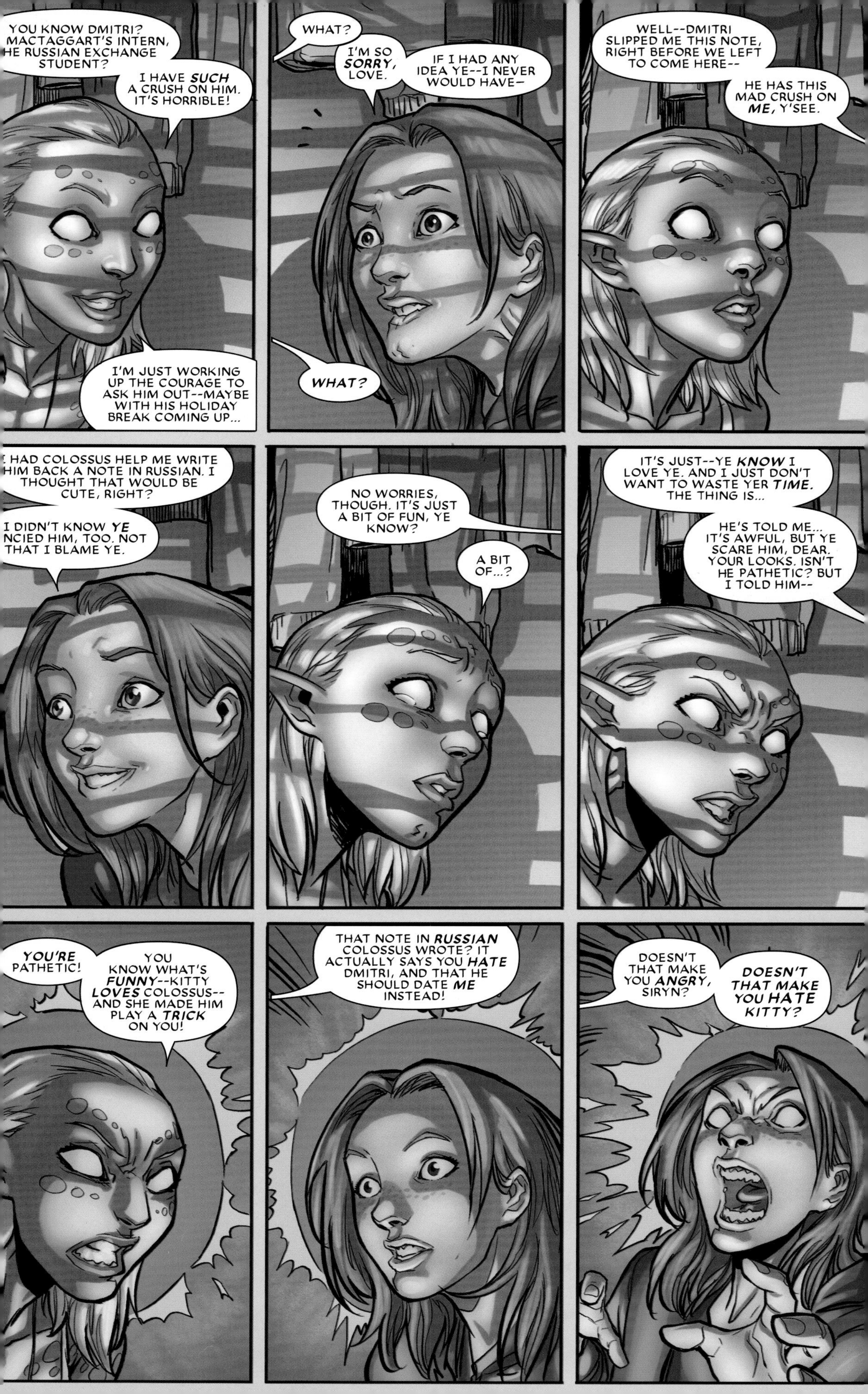
YOU KNOW DMITRI? MACTAGGART'S INTERN, HE RUSSIAN EXCHANGE STUDENT?
I HAVE SUCH A CRUSH ON HIM. IT'S HORRIBLE!
I'M JUST WORKING UP THE COURAGE TO ASK HIM OUT--MAYBE WITH HIS HOLIDAY BREAK COMING UP...
WHAT?
I'M SO SORRY, LOVE.
IF I HAD ANY IDEA YE--I NEVER WOULD HAVE--
WHAT?
WELL--DMITRI SLIPPED ME THIS NOTE, RIGHT BEFORE WE LEFT TO COME HERE--
HE HAS THIS MAD CRUSH ON ME, Y'SEE.
I HAD COLOSSUS HELP ME WRITE HIM BACK A NOTE IN RUSSIAN. I THOUGHT THAT WOULD BE CUTE, RIGHT?
I DIDN'T KNOW YE NCIED HIM, TOO. NOT THAT I BLAME YE.
NO WORRIES, THOUGH. IT'S JUST A BIT OF FUN, YE KNOW?
A BIT OF...?
IT'S JUST--YE KNOW I LOVE YE. AND I JUST DON'T WANT TO WASTE YER TIME. THE THING IS...
HE'S TOLD ME... IT'S AWFUL, BUT YE SCARE HIM, DEAR. YOUR LOOKS. ISN'T HE PATHETIC? BUT I TOLD HIM--
YOU'RE PATHETIC!
YOU KNOW WHAT'S FUNNY--KITTY LOVES COLOSSUS--AND SHE MADE HIM PLAY A TRICK ON YOU!
THAT NOTE IN RUSSIAN COLOSSUS WROTE? IT ACTUALLY SAYS YOU HATE DMITRI, AND THAT HE SHOULD DATE ME INSTEAD!
DOESN'T THAT MAKE YOU ANGRY, SIRYN?
DOESN'T THAT MAKE YOU HATE KITTY?

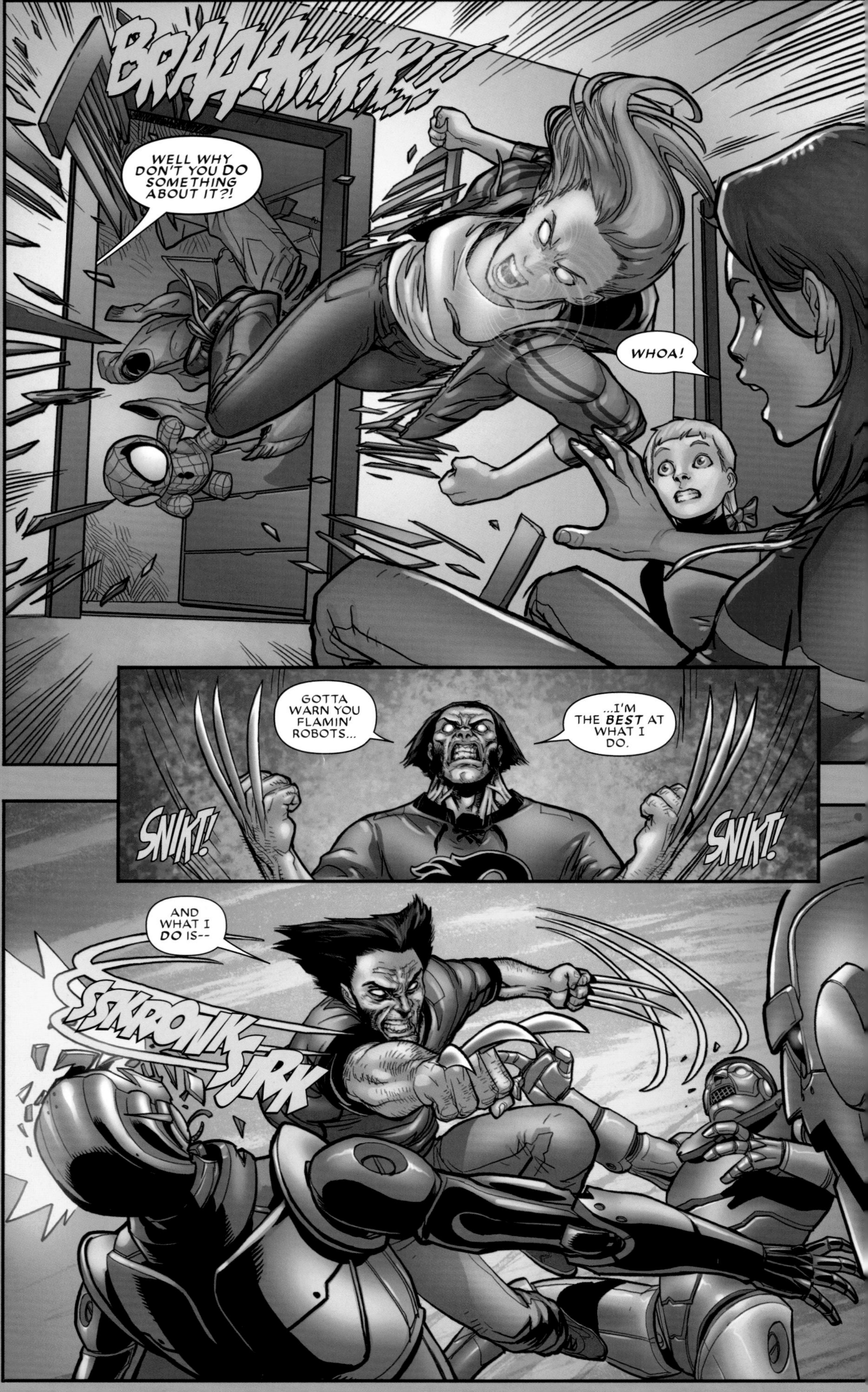
BRAAAKKKK!!!
WELL WHY DON'T YOU DO SOMETHING ABOUT IT?!
WHOA!
GOTTA WARN YOU FLAMIN' ROBOTS...
...I'M THE BEST AT WHAT I DO.
SNIKT!
SNIKT!
AND WHAT I DO IS--
SSKRONK
SHRK

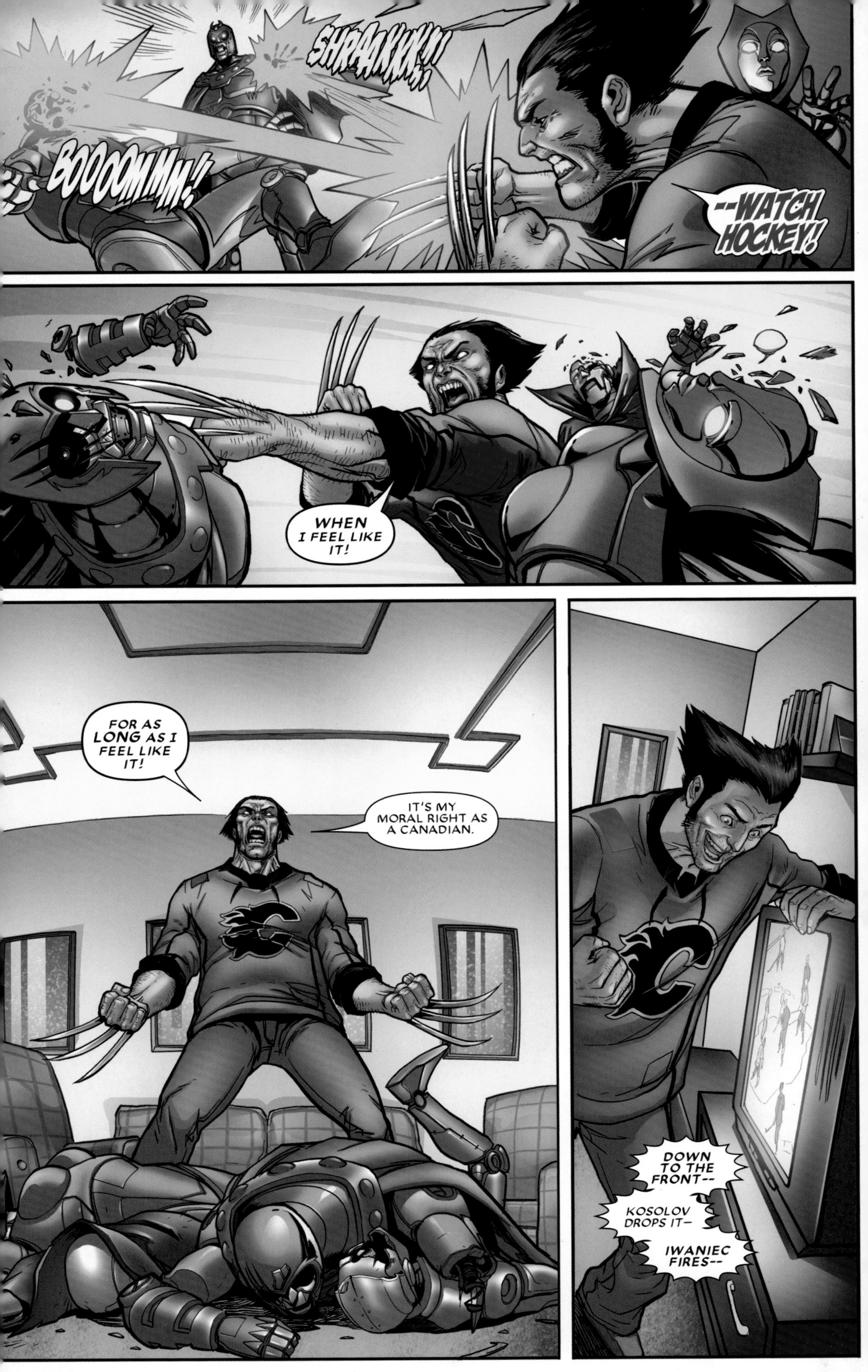
SHRAAKKK!!
BOOOOMMM!!
--WATCH HOCKEY!
WHEN I FEEL LIKE IT!
FOR AS LONG AS I FEEL LIKE IT!
IT'S MY MORAL RIGHT AS A CANADIAN.
DOWN TO THE FRONT--
KOSOLOV DROPS IT--
IWANIEC FIRES--

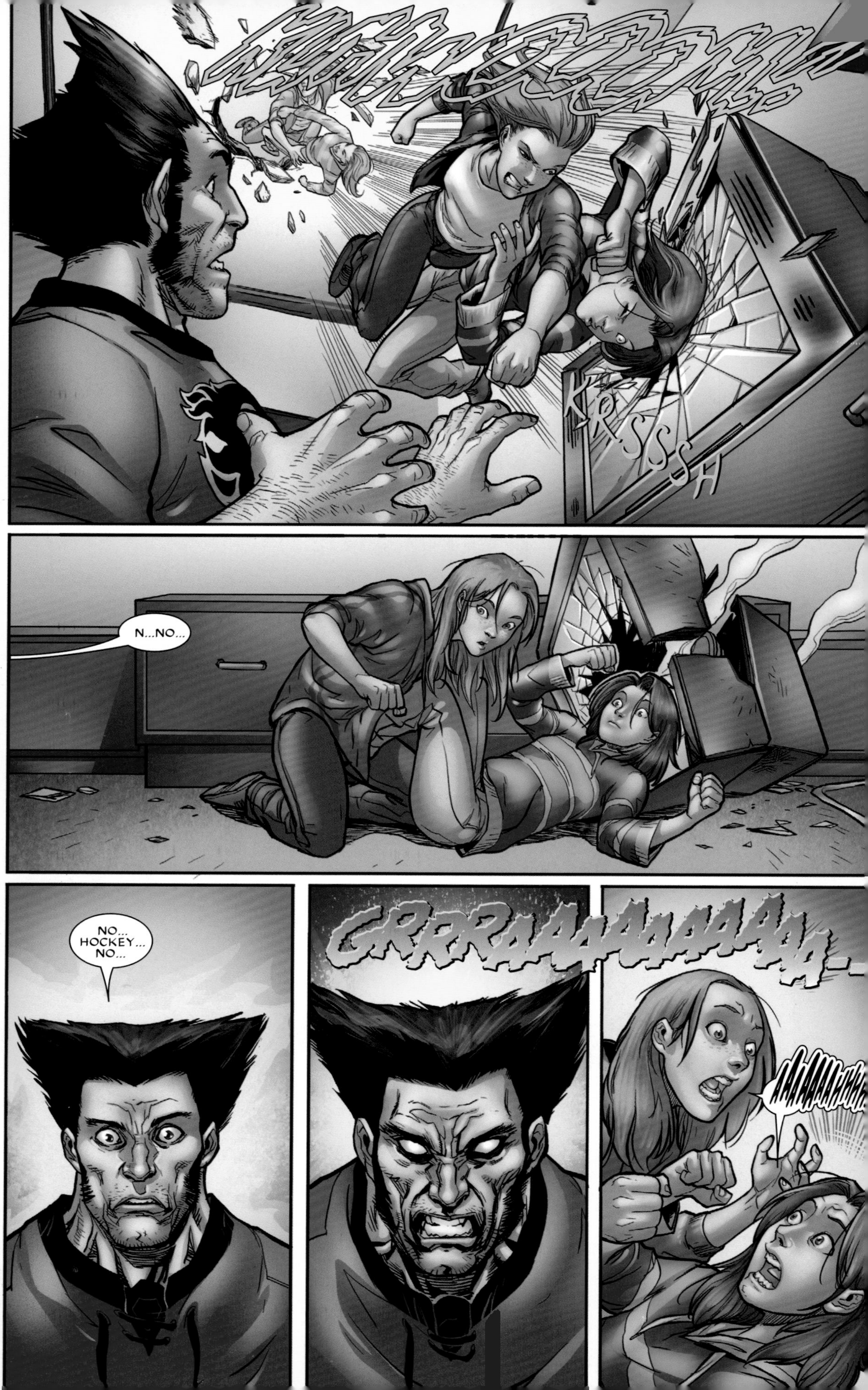
KRSSSH
N...NO...
NO...
HOCKEY...
NO...
GRRRAAAAAAAAAA--

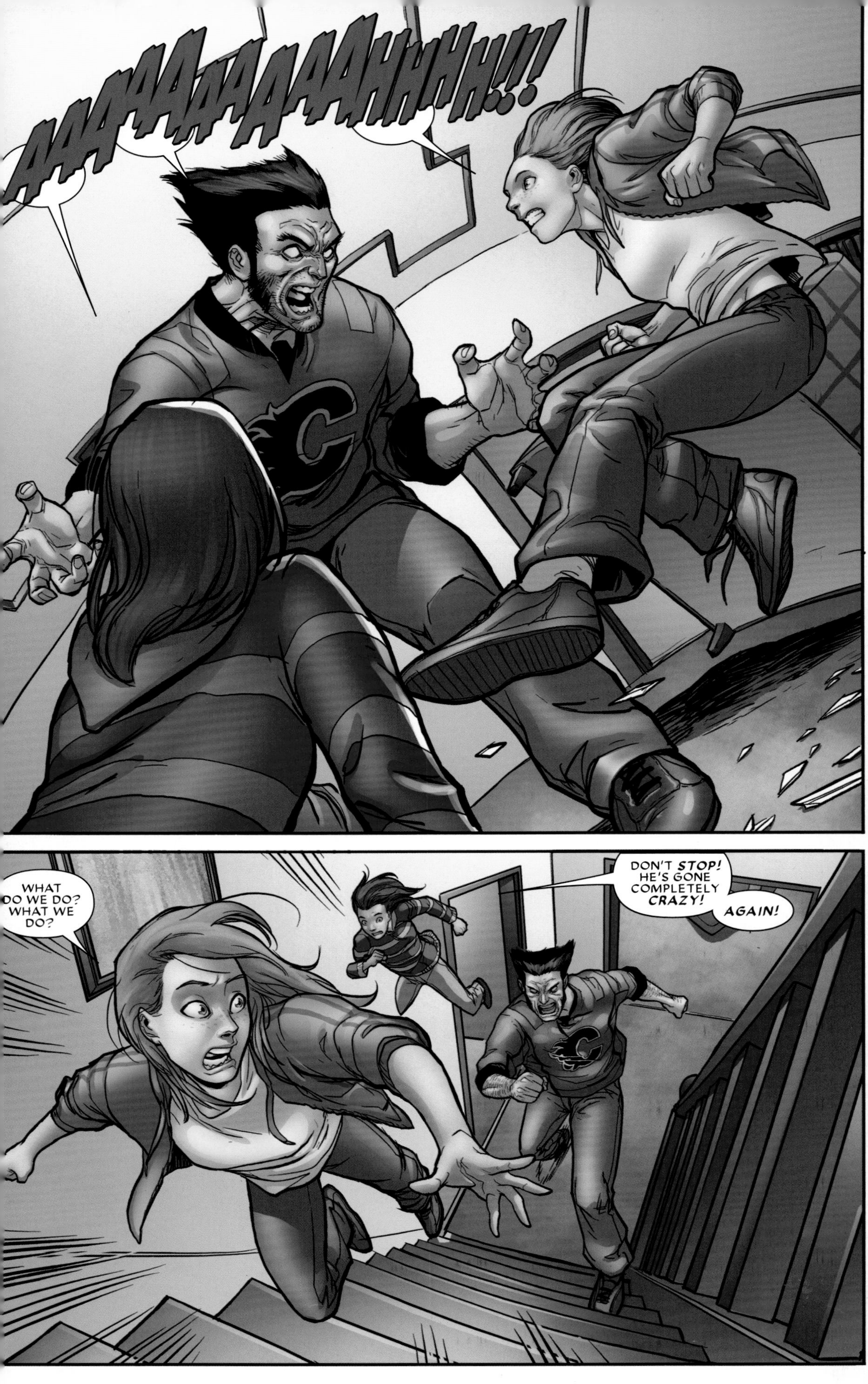
AAAAAAAAAAAAHHHHH!!!
WHAT DO WE DO? WHAT WE DO?
DON'T STOP! HE'S GONE COMPLETELY CRAZY!
AGAIN!

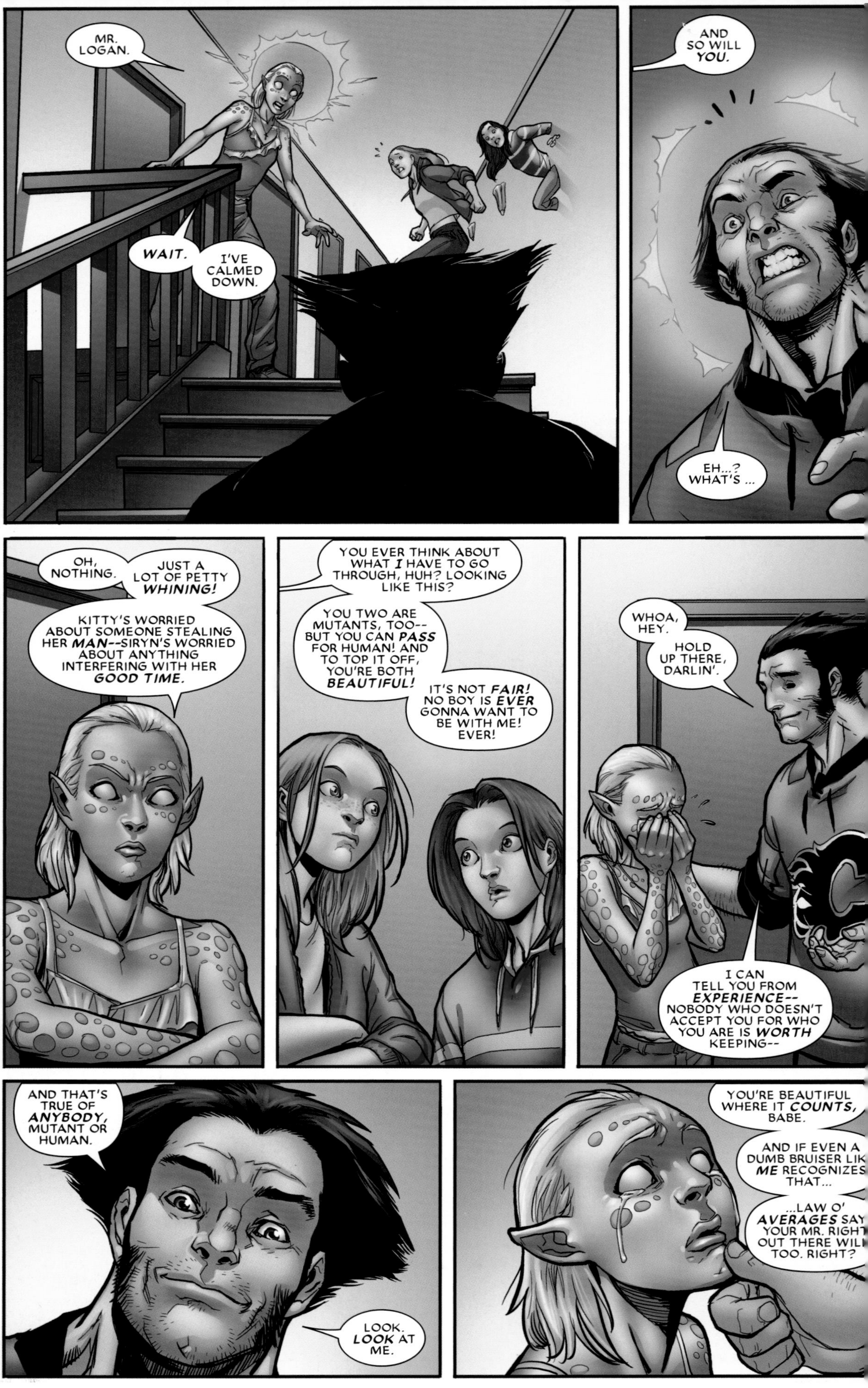

MR. LOGAN.
WAIT.
I'VE CALMED DOWN.
AND SO WILL YOU.
EH...? WHAT'S ...
OH, NOTHING.
JUST A LOT OF PETTY WHINING!
KITTY'S WORRIED ABOUT SOMEONE STEALING HER MAN--SIRYN'S WORRIED ABOUT ANYTHING INTERFERING WITH HER GOOD TIME.
YOU EVER THINK ABOUT WHAT I HAVE TO GO THROUGH, HUH? LOOKING LIKE THIS?
YOU TWO ARE MUTANTS, TOO--BUT YOU CAN PASS FOR HUMAN! AND TO TOP IT OFF, YOU'RE BOTH BEAUTIFUL!
IT'S NOT FAIR! NO BOY IS EVER GONNA WANT TO BE WITH ME! EVER!
WHOA, HEY.
HOLD UP THERE, DARLIN'.
I CAN TELL YOU FROM EXPERIENCE--NOBODY WHO DOESN'T ACCEPT YOU FOR WHO YOU ARE IS WORTH KEEPING--
AND THAT'S TRUE OF ANYBODY, MUTANT OR HUMAN.
LOOK. LOOK AT ME.
YOU'RE BEAUTIFUL WHERE IT COUNTS, BABE.
AND IF EVEN A DUMB BRUISER LIK ME RECOGNIZES THAT...
...LAW O' AVERAGES SAY YOUR MR. RIGHT OUT THERE WIL TOO. RIGHT?

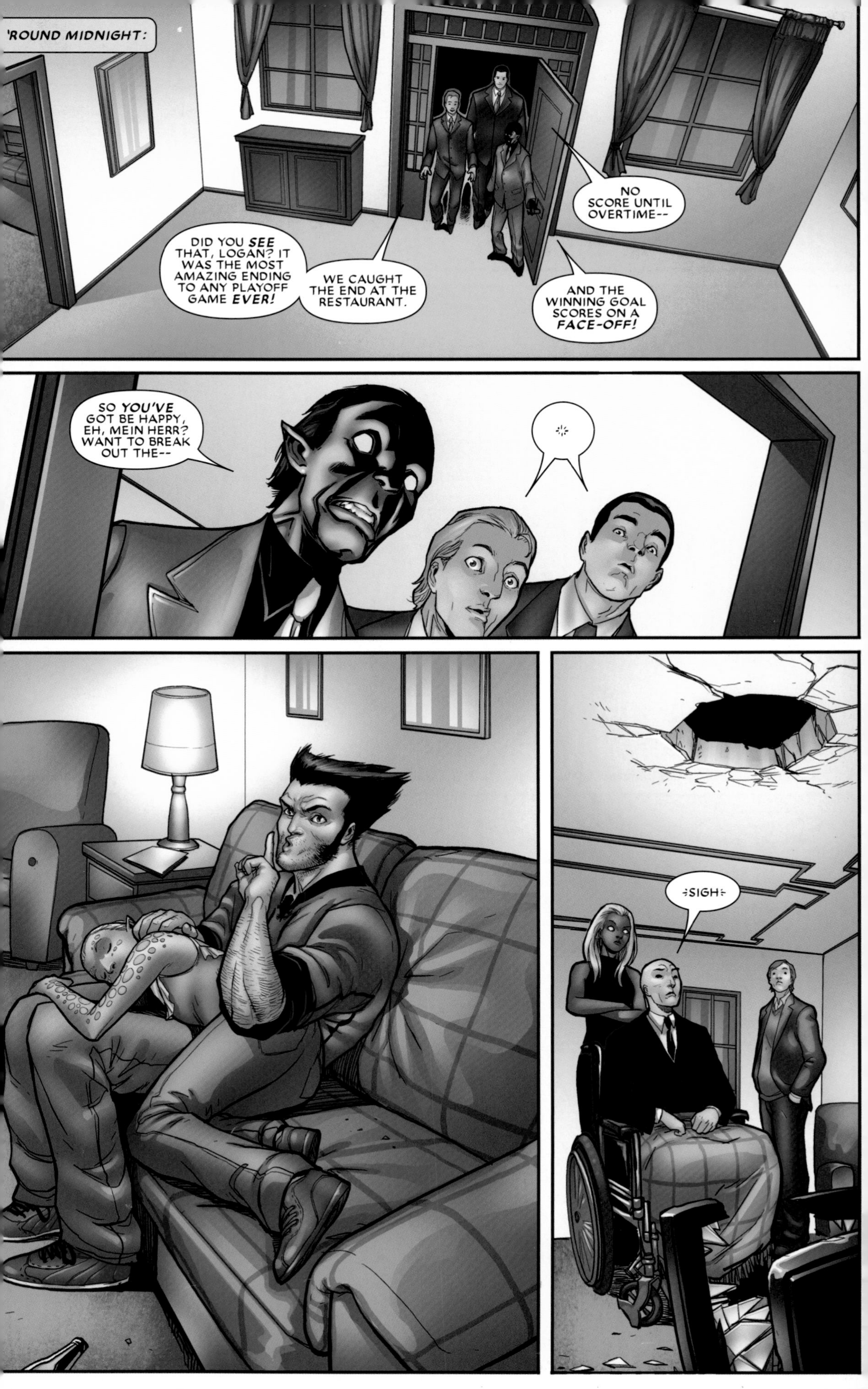
'ROUND MIDNIGHT:
DID YOU *SEE* THAT, LOGAN? IT WAS THE MOST AMAZING ENDING TO ANY PLAYOFF GAME *EVER!*
WE CAUGHT THE END AT THE RESTAURANT.
NO SCORE UNTIL OVERTIME--
AND THE WINNING GOAL SCORES ON A *FACE-OFF!*
SO *YOU'VE* GOT BE HAPPY, EH, MEIN HERR? WANT TO BREAK OUT THE--
=SIGH=

THE NEXT MORNING:

AGAIN-- I COULDN'T BE SORRIER, AMP.

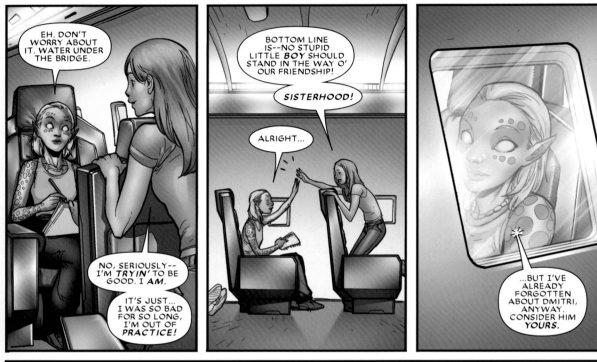

EH. DON'T WORRY ABOUT IT. WATER UNDER THE BRIDGE.

NO, SERIOUSLY-- I'M *TRYIN'* TO BE GOOD. I *AM*.

IT'S JUST... I WAS SO BAD FOR SO LONG, I'M OUT OF *PRACTICE!*

BOTTOM LINE IS--NO STUPID LITTLE *BOY* SHOULD STAND IN THE WAY O' OUR FRIENDSHIP!

SISTERHOOD!

ALRIGHT...

...BUT I'VE ALREADY FORGOTTEN ABOUT DMITRI, ANYWAY. CONSIDER HIM *YOURS.*

I'VE MOVED ON TO BIGGER AND BETTER PROSPECTS...